Acting Edition

I0591877

The Gradient

by Steph Del Rosso

FOR PRODUCTION INQUIRIES

UNITED STATES AND CANADA
info@concordtheatricals.com
1-866-979-0447

UNITED KINGDOM AND EUROPE
licensing@concordtheatricals.co.uk
020-7054-7298

Each title is subject to availability from Concord Theatricals Corp.,
depending upon country of performance. Please be aware that *THE
GRADIENT* may not be licensed by Concord Theatricals Corp. in
your territory. Professional and amateur producers should contact the
nearest Concord Theatricals Corp. office or licensing partner to verify
availability.

THE GRADIENT was originally produced by the Repertory Theatre of St. Louis (Hana S. Sharif, Artistic Director; Mark Bernstein, Managing Director). The performance was directed by Amelia Acosta Powell, with sets by Carolyn Mraz, costumes by Raquel Barretto, lighting by Mextly Couzin, projection design by Kaitlyn Pietras and Jason H. Thompson, sound by Sadah Espii Proctor, associate direction by Jaz Hall, dramaturgy by Sarah Slight, associate scenic design by Ant Ma, assistant direction by Aurora Behlke, and casting by JZ Casting. The production stage manager was Shannon Sturgis, and the assistant stage manager was Carolyn Ivy Carter. The cast was as follows:

TESS	Stephanie Machado
NATALIA / A VERY SOOTHING VOICE	Christina Acosta Robinson
JACKSON	Yousof Sultani
LOUIS	William DeMeritt
CLIENTS 1-8	Stephen Cefalu

THE GRADIENT was originally commissioned by Studio Theatre, Washington, D.C. (David Muse, Artistic Director; Rebecca Ende Lichtenberg, Managing Director).

THE GRADIENT was developed by Victory Gardens Theater, Chicago, Illinois (Chay Yew, Artistic Director; Erica Daniels, Executive Director) as part of the IGNITION Festival of New Plays 2019.

CHARACTERS

TESS – new to the job

NATALIA – old hat at the job

JACKSON – a client

LOUIS – a potential ally

CLIENTS 1-8 – a montage of men

A VERY SOOTHING VOICE – voiced by the actor playing Natalia

SETTING

The interior of a pristine office building.

TIME

A not-so-distant future.

AUTHOR'S NOTES

/ indicates when the next line begins.

[words in brackets] are unspoken.

(words in parentheses) are spoken under the breath.

Things move fast. Periods at the end of a sentence are the exception, not the norm. Transitions are instantaneous.

Caps in the Middle of a Sentence are meant for emphasis.

The men in this play are real. Do not turn them into caricatures.

1.

(Lights.)

*(**NATALIA** immediately enters and begins speaking.)*

(She moves fast. Keep up.)

NATALIA. So the kitchen and snack room are there

TESS. Got it

NATALIA. Bathrooms there – with showers, which you might need if you're doing a double

TESS. Got it

NATALIA. Plus the body wash they've been stocking the shelves with is incredible – some kind of shea butter goji berry I don't even know, I feel like I'm at a spa

TESS. Wow / that's

NATALIA. Client pods are in the north wing, client session rooms are in the south wing and client breakout rooms are in the west wing. Which means right now we're in the...

> *(**TESS** doesn't know.)*

East wing. *(Hopes the answer is no.)* Do you need me to walk you through all that again?

TESS. No no, I'll figure it out

NATALIA. Good. Down the hall is where all your intake gets uploaded, around the corner is where all your incremental tests get uploaded. Don't confuse them

1

TESS. Intake, incremental. Got it

NATALIA. Other way around

TESS. Incremental, intake

NATALIA. Right. The coffee on our floor sucks – we're working on it – but in the meantime you can use the machine in the lobby, it's way better

TESS. Good to / know

NATALIA. Two days a week these Silicon Valley bros take over the space next door. They're trying to build some device that erases the part of your brain that compares yourself to other people

TESS. That / sounds [?]

NATALIA. They do catered lunch whenever they're here and it's surprisingly easy to snag their leftovers so I would try that. Don't get me wrong I love Roxane but sometimes I don't want a flaxseed smoothie I want like, a steak

TESS. Who's / [Roxane]

NATALIA. Roxane? Our chef. Oh and my name's Dr. Acosta but you can call me Natalia. Did I forget to say that? You're probably thinking who the hell is this person

TESS. No I remember from orientation: "Hi I'm Natalia and I brought Nothing to the picnic." I was like: great, she hates name games as much as I do

NATALIA. I've been telling HR to update those icebreakers for months

TESS. *(A joke.)* Maybe we can start a campaign

NATALIA. *(Not really into the joke.)* Maybe.

There are roundtables, panel discussions, happy hours, themed parties, and themed brunches. I would recommend attending as many as you can, as often as you can, at least at first. It probably sounds overwhelming / but

TESS. Not overwhelming at all. It's refreshing that everyone wants to build community

NATALIA. Yes and no. We're not exactly kum-bay-ya. Just, collaborative

TESS. At my last job we only got together when someone retired. A lot of people hated each other over there

NATALIA. Well no one seemed to hate you. You came highly recommended.

TESS. Really?

NATALIA. You sound surprised. You do realize this isn't an interview, right? You already got the job?

TESS. Ha! No I know. I know. That place just wasn't big on validation

(Slightly awkward beat.)

*(**NATALIA** also isn't big on validation...)*

Plus, it was hard to tell what kind of impact I was making when I spent most of my time alone

in a basement

holding a pipette

*(**NATALIA** brightens.)*

NATALIA. Academia, right? So inefficient and abstract. It's like: I don't care about your "studies." Where are your results?

TESS. Exactly! I actually didn't just remember your name from the icebreaker. You and Dr. Quill and Dr. Foggstein were basically, celebrities. At my lab.

NATALIA. *(Kind of loving this.)* I'm sure that's not true

TESS. I'm serious. You beat us all to the punch! You literally Found a Cure for men's / toxic

NATALIA. Not exclusively men

TESS. *(Whoops.)* Oh, / yes

NATALIA. Primarily men, but not exclusively

TESS. Right. You found a cure for – people's toxic behavior. We were kicking ourselves. Of course, an algorithm. Of COURSE

NATALIA. Remind me, what was the focus of your research?

TESS. We were comparing the brainwaves and hormones of male and female mice

NATALIA. *(Amateur hour.)* Ah, sure. Nice idea

TESS. It seemed So groundbreaking

Until it didn't

NATALIA. I'd make sure you're extremely familiar with the algorithm, since it's a bit different from your previous line of work

TESS. *(Reciting.)* Grade on the empathy scale plus grade on the vulnerability scale times rate of introspection times externalized guilt divided by number of transgressions raised to the power of potential for growth

NATALIA. You memorized it.

TESS. I did.

NATALIA. *(...)* We pride ourselves on innovation here, not necessarily, regurgitation. Is that going to be an adjustment for you?

TESS. *(Deflated...)* Oh. Definitely not. I'm All about innovation

NATALIA. Well. We'll keep tracking that.

What else what else, let's see... Always press the green button at the sign-in station, even after the fingerprinting and the full-body scan – otherwise you won't officially be logged in. And you do Not have to mentor the interns. They'll try to suck up to you but you have no obligation to work with them, that's Mandy's problem

TESS. *(Trying to remember who that is.)* Mandy –

NATALIA. Dr. Foggstein. She'll be Mandy to you eventually.

So: you've got your first set of intakes this morning. You ready?

TESS. Yes?

NATALIA. Is that a question?

TESS. *(Trying again.)* Yes

NATALIA. Still sounded like a question. Try to self-correct that, okay?

TESS. Sorry

NATALIA. Try to self-correct that too: over-apologizing

TESS. *(Almost says sorry.)* Absolutely

NATALIA. It's Monday, so we've got a Lot of new clients. Just remember: when you're in there, you're in charge. And I don't mean that in some ra ra empowerment way – I mean you're Literally the authority in that room. Don't let them call the shots. YOU call the shots in there

TESS. I call the shots, right

NATALIA. Don't let them boss you around. And don't let them charm you either. Do NOT become their friends. And I mean it's ridiculous I have to say this but based on past experience I have to say this: Do Not Enter a Relationship with them

(This makes **TESS** *crack up.)*

You laugh / but

TESS. Yeah, uh. That's not gonna happen. This is my dream job that is not gonna happen

NATALIA. Good.

>   (**NATALIA** *hands* **TESS** *an iPad and shakes her hand.*)

Tess, Welcome to The Gradient. We are so happy to have you.

TESS. Thrilled to be here.

>   (*They shake hands.* **TESS** *beams.*)

NATALIA. Smile

TESS. What

>   (*Camera flash.*)

>   (*Mid-handshake,* **NATALIA** *flashes a radiant smile.*)

>   (**TESS** *looks kind of flustered and awkward.*)

>   (*The handshake ends.*)

NATALIA. For the website

TESS. (*...Shit.*) Oh cool

NATALIA. You'll be in Room Four.

TESS. Room / [?]

>   (*Lights snap to Room Four.*)

>   (**NATALIA** *vanishes.*)

>   (*An asterisk * means we snap to a new client.*)

>   (*There should be some kind of crisp physical shift. Things move fast.*)

>   (*It's like a Shitty Dude Ballet.*)

(We're in the middle of –)

CLIENT 1. *(Ivy League douche.)* – And I like saying the word cunt. I enjoy saying the word cunt. That's My Right, that's my individual liberty, And I'm gonna use it! Because I Enjoy /

TESS. Saying it, yes I got that

CLIENT 1. We cannot condone censorship – I will NOT condone censorship

TESS. Okay, let's talk about the circumstances in which this word was / used

CLIENT 1. The circumstances were me, a grown-ass, independent man, making a grown-ass, independent decision about the language I use – the language I choose to Re-Claim

TESS. Let's linger on "re-claim" for just a /

CLIENT 1. *(!!)* I am Allowed To Say / –

  *

CLIENT 2. *(Surfer bro.)* Yeahhhhhhh so that's when I was working for this private catering company for like three, four months and I would say, like I would say the work life and the social life at that place was pretty like. Pretty like. Fluid

TESS. Could you clarify that please?

CLIENT 2. Yeahhhhhhh I mean look, I would say like

Yeah. Basically. Like. Yeah. Fluid.

TESS. Okay, could you – could you maybe use a different /

  *

CLIENT 3. *(Tough dude.)* I don't understand what you're implying

TESS.   I'm just asking if you could relay an incident involving a woman who lives in your building

CLIENT 3. An "incident"?

TESS. On the night of /

CLIENT 3. What are you a cop

(Cop voice.) "Where were you on the night of –"

You sound like a cop

TESS. I'm

so sorry to give you that impression

CLIENT 3. (Fucking bullshit.)

TESS. *(...)* Maybe we should start over

CLIENT 3. (This is truly fucking /)

*

TESS. *(?)* So that's a no, you didn't intend to cause harm

(**CLIENT 4** *shakes his head.*)

(...?) No, you Did intend to cause harm

(**CLIENT 4** *shakes his head.*)

Okay, so the first one

(**CLIENT 4** *does nothing.*)

Any interest in elaborating on that?

(**CLIENT 4** *shakes his head.*)

Gotcha. That's

Great. Cool. Great

*

CLIENT 5. *(Distinguished older gentleman.)* I guess I'd say I feel disheartened. I worry about my sons. I'm a loving father of two. Two boys

TESS. That sounds nice

CLIENT 5. I just hope, I just hope and pray, that their future shakes out differently

TESS. *(We're getting somewhere...!)* And how would you like it to be different?

CLIENT 5. Well, first and foremost, I want my boys to feel... safe

TESS. Safe...

CLIENT 5. Protected from this terrifying culture

TESS. Uh-huh...

CLIENT 5. Where men are Denied the Benefit of the Doubt!

＊

CLIENT 6. *(Mr. Nice Guy.)* Look, we're on the same team here

TESS. I agree

CLIENT 6. I totally defer to you. I want to follow your rules, I want to be as respectful and courteous as possible

TESS. That's, great to hear

CLIENT 6. But I also want to,

Like juuuuust so we have everything out on the table I want to bring an, item – if you will – to your attention. An item I find, relevant

TESS. Oh. Okay

CLIENT 6. It's in the "anatomy" category. Cuz I'm kindaaaa a science guy

TESS. *(...)* You don't say

CLIENT 6. So. Yeah. I would be remiss, you know, if I didn't mention. The issue of Blue balls

TESS. The issue of /

CLIENT 6. Blue balls. For your consideration. As they are, anatomically speaking, a crucial factor that should not be discounted when we evaluate, you know, these types of issues.

Just spitballing, we can always adjust the language – again, I Totally defer to you but,

I'd like for you to include that in my file.

> (**TESS** *swallows.*)

TESS. That's not actually a thing.

CLIENT 6. Excuse me

TESS. Blue balls

is not a thing

CLIENT 6. *(What the ?)* Um /

TESS. *(Big smile.)* Moving on

> *

CLIENT 7. *(Hyperventilating.)* I just feel *(Breath.)* like *(Breath.)* I've been *(Breath.)* mischaracterized! And I just I just I just

> (**CLIENT 7** *breathes shallowly.*)

TESS. Okay, sir /

CLIENT 7. *(Spiraling.)* And sure okay sure *(Breath.)* maybe I did some things I regret but I didn't *(Breath.)* think *(Breath.)* it *(Breath.)* would *(Breath.)* come *(Breath.)* to *(Breath!!!)* /

TESS. SIR!

> (**CLIENT 7** *stops.*)

I'm going to need you to take one deep breath in

And one deep breath out

(**CLIENT 7** *does as he's told.*)

CLIENT 7. *(Relaxed.)* That felt /

   *

CLIENT 8. *(Super chill, chewing gum.)* But you know man, *You Know*

TESS. *(?)* What do I Know

CLIENT 8. You know that there's murder, and then there's manslaughter. Felony, misdemeanor. Pancakes, bacon. Right?

TESS. You had me and then that last / one

CLIENT 8. Everyone's got their shit. I have my shit, You have your shit, that lady who checked me in has her shit. But on the shit spectrum, I guarantee you we're all doing Pretty Well for ourselves

TESS. You have a

   lot of faith in humanity

CLIENT 8. I'm just sayin', what's this all about, you know? All this noise? Why are we Here

TESS. *(Even.)* You're here because this is The Gradient

CLIENT 8. *(Dumbass...)* Yeah, I've noticed

TESS. Not prison.

CLIENT 8. Okay but /

TESS. So consider yourself lucky.

   *

      (**TESS** *looks exhausted. But also kind of amped. Buzzing.*)

      (*Long day, but she stayed afloat.*)

      (*Maybe she takes a gulp of coffee.*)

A VERY SOOTHING VOICE. Excellent work today, Tess. Please report to Room Seven for your final client intake with /

JACKSON. Jackson Cuthbert.

(Lights snap.)

(A room with **TESS** *and* **JACKSON.***)*

TESS. *(Consulting notes.)* Can you please verify your identification number for me?

JACKSON. 5247

TESS. Thank you, #5247. I'm going to start with some basic biographical questions. Can you please describe your first romantic relationship?

JACKSON. Wow we really just Dive In. I figured you'd throw me a softball before we, dug up my past relationships

TESS. We've got a lot of ground to cover.

*(***TESS*** waits.)*

JACKSON. Okay okay. Keely-May Langdon. My babysitter when I was ten.

We're talking, unreciprocated relationship here

TESS. So this was a crush

JACKSON. *(No.)* That always felt kind of second-rate, as a term. I was pretty swoony. Like I was pretty far in

TESS. Any specific Keely-May memories?

*(***JACKSON*** considers. Then lights up.)*

JACKSON. She was really good at video, stuff. We would make all these, short films when she was babysitting me. Not like, "films," but. Well we did this one that was a magic show? And I wore this plastic top hat and I'd go, "I am going to disappear now." And then she'd stop recording and I'd run out of the frame, so it looked like I had [disappeared]

TESS. Got it.

JACKSON. We took it to Sundance. Didn't win the Oscar but, it was still an honor to be nominated.

> *(**JACKSON** waits for **TESS** to play along or laugh. She doesn't.)*

(Considering her.) You've got quite the poker face

TESS. It's, just my face

(Moving right along.) How about your first serious relationship?

JACKSON. Probably Shelley Freemont? College. I made her a Valentine's Day playlist – that felt serious. Felt like this Grand Gesture. You know, Elliott Smith. Lots of Radiohead

> *(**TESS** jots this down. **JACKSON** considers her.)*

You hate that

TESS. Radiohead?

JACKSON. The whole concept of a Valentine's Day playlist, I bet you hate that. Way too on the nose for you.

TESS. I'm not judging your responses, I'm just recording them for the algorithm

JACKSON. No way. You're definitely making fun of me in your head right now

TESS. Well. Agree to disagree

JACKSON. Rose petals on the floor, you hate that

TESS. If you say so

JACKSON. Sunset serenades – the worst

TESS. Never really crossed my mind

JACKSON. *(I've got it.)* Oh oh! Girls who dream up how they'll get proposed to, you *can't stand* them.

(*Brief beat as* **TESS** *clocks that he is exactly right.*)

(*But then:*)

TESS. You should say "women"

JACKSON. What

TESS. You should say "women" instead of girls. Okay?

JACKSON. Oh. Okay. Got it.

TESS. Let's return to Shelley. Was she your first sexual relationship?

JACKSON. No that was Maya Huang. High school

TESS. Do you have any specific Maya memories?

(**JACKSON** *considers.*)

JACKSON. She wore this tank top sometimes, this like loose-fitting tank top. And she knew it was loose so she wore another tank top underneath, like an undershirt-y thing. But that was loose too. So she was just a girl wearing two loose tank tops.

(**TESS** *writes this down.*)

(*Shit.*) I said girl again

TESS. Any other Maya memories, other than her...clothing?

JACKSON. Oh. Talking about her tank top probably sounded

Bad. Didn't it

TESS. Well it didn't sound great

JACKSON. (*Backpedaling.*) That time is foggy, honestly. I was like, all hormones. I slept around a lot in high school, but I still think that's better than pretending you're a functioning enough human at seventeen to actually have a meaningful relationship with anybody Can I have some –

(TESS pours JACKSON water.)

(As she pours.) They seem like they run a tight ship around here. You must be exhausted

TESS. I'll get used to it

JACKSON. *(Intrigued.)* Wait – are you new? Oh man, am I your first client?

TESS. No. / No

JACKSON. I'm totally your first client

TESS. No you're Really not

JACKSON. I feel honored

(TESS writes something down.)

Uh-oh, what did I do? You just wrote something down, but you didn't ask me a question. What did you just write down?

TESS. I'm not authorized to tell you that

JACKSON. "Authorized." You guys are All Business around here. The people who checked me in this morning were basically robots

TESS. ...Well that's because some of us Are robots.

JACKSON. Wait what?

TESS. We're about 50/50 humans, bots

JACKSON. How can you. Tell them apart?

TESS. ...I'm messing with you.

(JACKSON laughs.)

JACKSON. Okay, okay, there we go! Some personality

TESS. *(Back to business.)* Can you please describe the first time you learned that your sexuality could be used as a tool?

JACKSON. I'm not sure I follow

TESS. The first time you learned that your sexuality could, get you something that you wanted

JACKSON. When is sexuality ever Not linked to getting you something that you wanted

TESS. We're interested in when you made that discovery

JACKSON. Uhhhh

Probably middle school. The "fall formal." First time I ever grinded with girls. And then later that night: first time I was invited to Mike McLachlan's house. Like clockwork.

TESS. I'm guessing Mike was hot shit?

JACKSON. He was king

(TESS *marks this down.*)

What about you

TESS. What

JACKSON. When's the first time *you* realized sexuality could be a tool? Throwing it back

TESS. Sure sure

JACKSON. Lobbing it back your way

TESS. Clearly we're not talking about me right now

JACKSON. It's not like I'm gonna use it against you. I think it might actually help me. If you open up, I open up. Like therapy

TESS. That's not how therapy works

JACKSON. Come on. I'm genuinely curious

TESS. Not a word I would use to describe you

JACKSON. Curious?

TESS. Genuine.

JACKSON. Are you calling me a liar?

TESS. That's not what I said

JACKSON. It's kind of what you said

TESS. *(Psh.)* I did not use the word liar

JACKSON. But I thought you were only supposed to Record my responses, not make judgments.

TESS. *(Psh.)* What, are you going to report me?

JACKSON. Depends. Is that an option?

TESS. *(...)* If, a client thinks it's necessary

JACKSON. Okay so yes. I'd like to report you.

TESS. You'd like to / [??]

JACKSON. What's the protocol for that?

TESS. Um –

> *(**TESS** freezes. Is this seriously happening?)*

JACKSON. Oh my god, I'm kidding. I'm kidding! Payback for your whole robot thing

TESS. *(Forced.)* Ha. You got me

JACKSON. Oh shit you look kind of spooked

TESS. I'm fine

JACKSON. Did I really freak you out?

TESS. I'm fine, let's / return to

JACKSON. I was just kidding /

TESS. *(Back to the questionnaire.)* Tell me about a woman in your life you admire

JACKSON. Everyone says their mom, don't they? Their mom or like, Mother Teresa?

TESS. I can't disclose other clients' answers

> (**JACKSON** *briefly considers.*)

JACKSON. *(Matter-of-fact.)* I admire You. For this work

TESS. *(?)* You're supposed to name someone in your life. As in your life Outside of here

JACKSON. Well Here is still life. Each breath we take is a part of our journey. So. My answer's you

> (**TESS** *tries to hold it together. And then – she cracks up.*)

TESS. I'm sorry – "Each breath we take is a part of our journey"? Was that the uh, name of your Valentine's Day playlist or –?

JACKSON. Yeah that was pretty fucking cheesy wasn't it

TESS. Maybe indie rock is your next big thing. That could be the title of your EP

JACKSON. And also the hit single

TESS. I'll get the marketing team on top of that

JACKSON. And I'll thank you first in my awards speech

TESS. Oh just thank the fans

JACKSON. Aren't you my biggest fan?

TESS. Used to be – then you got too commercial

JACKSON. Riiiight

TESS. Rookie mistake

> (*Brief beat. They've both been enjoying this bit.*)

JACKSON. Are all my sessions going to be this fun?

TESS. This

isn't really about having "fun"

JACKSON. Haven't hated it so far

TESS. *(Back to business.)* I think it would be best if we move to the most important question of the entire intake process

JACKSON. *(Jokey.)* Pressure. Is. On.

TESS. #5247, why are you here?

JACKSON. *(Jokey.)* Like, existentially?

TESS. You know I don't mean existentially

>   *(She waits.)*

The quicker we get through this, the quicker you can go back to your pod

JACKSON. But I can't joke around with my pod!

TESS. This isn't a [joke]

#5247, why are you at The Gradient?

>   *(JACKSON takes a breath.)*

JACKSON. Because

I misunderstood a situation. A situation in which I, completely unknowingly,

Pressured someone

But NOT physically. There was No Physical Force. Are you writing that down? Can you please write that down?

TESS. It says here that you proceeded to push her hand toward your genitals?

JACKSON. But not

forcefully

TESS. As well as her head?

JACKSON. *(Kind of freaking out.)* And then I stopped I'm not a maniac I stopped

TESS. Were you aware that she was not enjoying herself?

JACKSON. Absolutely not

TESS. Has anyone ever called you aggressive?

JACKSON. No

TESS. Former partners? Flings? Friends?

JACKSON. No

TESS. And what about you personally:

Would you, personally, describe yourself as aggressive?

> *(*JACKSON *takes a minute.)*

> *(Considers.)*

JACKSON. Would you?

> *(Darkness.)*

> *(And then* NATALIA, *in spotlight.)*

NATALIA. Welcome to The Gradient.

Tell me, what brings you here today? Did you happen to...cross a line? Misread a signal? Are you a fan of knees? Smalls of the back? That work holiday party that always "gets out of hand"? Relax! Relaaaaax. You seem a little, anxious. Why don't you take a deeeeeep breath. We get it. We get how much you love reminding others about "nuance" and "spectrums" and "gray areas." Here at The Gradient, "gray areas" are our specialty. Because we believe that all actions – even the "gray" ones – have consequences. In just three short years, The Gradient has rehabilitated 5,000 people who have committed sexual misconduct or assault. How, you ask? We've created an algorithm that mathematically and scientifically generates a personalized, comprehensive treatment plan, based on each client's unique background and needs. So tell us: How are you fucked up? And what's your capacity to change? Who are you now, and who are you capable of becoming? Go ahead. Have a seat. Someone will be with you shortly.

2.

(The next day. Late afternoon.)

*(**TESS** makes a fresh batch of coffee.)*

(Or. Tries to.)

(She struggles.)

(The machine is sputtering. Making weird beeping sounds.)

(She curses under her breath.)

*(**LOUIS** enters. Considers her.)*

LOUIS. You need some help?

TESS. Nope, I'm good!

LOUIS. It's finicky, / so

TESS. I'm good thanks!

LOUIS. Happens a lot, / but

TESS. Yeah I'm fine thank you though!

(Very weird, loud beeping gurgle sound.)

LOUIS. Kay.

*(**TESS** pours coffee.)*

(It dribbles out. She can barely fill half a cup.)

*(**LOUIS** looks at her. She looks back.)*

(She sips.)

TESS. *(Re: the coffee.)* Mhmmm.

LOUIS. I'm Louis

TESS. I remember, hey. I'm / [Tess]

LOUIS. Tess. "Brought tuna fish to the picnic." Bold choice, by the way. Smelly

TESS. Well. Brain food right?

LOUIS. Pretty sure that's just salmon

TESS. Pretty sure that's all fish

> (**TESS** *sips the shitty coffee.*)

LOUIS. How was day one?

TESS. *(Lying.)* Good. It was

Good

LOUIS. *(Knows she's lying.)* Mondays are always a slog. Today will seem easy by comparison. Don't worry

TESS. *(Lying...)* Oh yeah I'm not worried

> (**TESS** *reaches for a pair of Google Glass-like goggles and a joystick.*)
>
> (**LOUIS** *notices.*)

LOUIS. Ah. First data entry. Did Natalia give you the walk-through?

TESS. [No? Kind of?]

Yeah. She did. Yeah

LOUIS. She's not the most thorough, / so

TESS. I'm sure I'll get the hang of it

> (**TESS** *clicks a few buttons.*)
>
> *(Click.)*

ROBOT VOICE. Error

> *(Click.)*

Error

(Click.)

ROBOT VOICE. Error

> **(LOUIS** *watches* **TESS.***)*

> **(TESS** *will not look at* **LOUIS.***)*

> *(Click.)*

Error

TESS. (Shit)

LOUIS. ...How you doing

TESS. Awesome Doing awesome

ROBOT VOICE. Error

LOUIS. Sounds

Awesome

TESS. Just

learning on the job

LOUIS. Cool. Cool

ROBOT VOICE. Error

TESS. (Piece of /)

LOUIS. Hey. I don't want to, uh, overstep but. Can I just – Do you mind if I –

> **(LOUIS** *approaches* **TESS.***)*

> **(TESS** *finally looks at him.)*

> *(And then:)*

TESS. Yeah actually please. Thank you

> **(LOUIS** *puts on his own pair of goggles.)*

LOUIS. Okay, so first off: you're logged in as Guest not Staff

TESS. Oh, whoops

LOUIS. It's fine just scan your fingerprint right here and then

>   (**TESS** *does.*)

Boom. You're in. See that timestamp? That means it's storing all the data we've collected in the past seventy-two hours

TESS. Woah

LOUIS. Yeah. Don't accidentally press delete

TESS. Is that

possible?

LOUIS. *(Ominous.)* Anything's possible

TESS. ...What?

LOUIS. *(Laughing.)* I'm kidding. Okay, this is how client #5012 scored in each of the algorithm's categories. See the columns? Empathy, Vulnerability, Intro/spection

TESS. *(Reciting.)* Introspection, Externalized Guilt, Potential for Growth

LOUIS. *(Lightly making fun.)* Did you

memorize the algorithm?

TESS. *(Yes.)* No

LOUIS. Okay...

TESS. *(Admitting.)* Yeah. Yeah I did.

LOUIS. Wooow. We've got a superfan on our hands.

TESS. If someone had told my nerdy little high-school self a place like this was going to exist, she would have lost her mind

LOUIS. *(Sizing her up.)* Were you like a mathlete?

TESS. What?

LOUIS. High-schooler Tess, was she a mathlete

TESS. We didn't have that.

LOUIS. Quiz bowl then?

TESS. ...I won the science fair

LOUIS. I'm sorry you *won* the science fair?

TESS. *(A little proud, still?)* Twice

LOUIS. *(!)* Twice???

TESS. I also ate bagel bites with my friends and got drunk after prom, you know, normal things

LOUIS. And had a high-school sweetheart named...Trevor

TESS. What? No

LOUIS. *(Trying again.)* Miguel

TESS. No

LOUIS. *(Trying again.)* C.J.

TESS. *(Laughing.)* Uh, no

LOUIS. Named...

> *(TESS makes an empty hands gesture.)*

TESS. I've got nothing. Late bloomer

LOUIS. *(Sizing her up anew?)* Huh. Interesting

TESS. *(Re: the screen.)* Wait what's that?

LOUIS. Oh, superfan's got a question?

TESS. *(Not unkindly.)* Don't call me that

LOUIS. That's this client's public announcement that they're headed to The Gradient. Their potential for growth score always increases if they formally announce they're coming. And don't forget to check their payment information, another score boost if they've paid out of pocket to be here

TESS. Wait why?

LOUIS. Shows initiative

TESS. *(...)* But does it?

LOUIS. What else would it show

TESS. ...That they're loaded

LOUIS. Well yeah, that too. But no surprise there

So once you log their scores, it's time to input them into the algorithm. Which means...

(**LOUIS** *clicks some buttons on the joystick.*)

ROBOT VOICE. Drama Therapy

LOUIS. They receive the first step of their personalized treatment program

TESS. *(!)* Woah. That's amazing

LOUIS. We like to think so

TESS. All right let me try

(**TESS** *drags the files as instructed by* **LOUIS**, *with her joystick.*)

(*Click click click.*)

(*And then:*)

ROBOT VOICE. Memory Inventory

LOUIS. There you go!

(**TESS** *tries another.*)

ROBOT VOICE. Step Inside Their Shoes

LOUIS. Nice, you've got this

TESS. Wait, is that number how many I have left?

LOUIS. Unfortunately...yes

TESS. *(Trying...)* Oh. Okay. Cool.

LOUIS. It helps if you

make a little dance out of it

TESS. *(...?)* Uh, what

LOUIS. Like

>*(**LOUIS** demonstrates.)*

>*(He does a bit where he clicks the joystick rhythmically, bopping around like he's a DJ.)*

>*(Maybe he "sings" along with the computer sounds? Maybe he pretends he's at a club??)*

(Doing a bit.) Click drag click drag toggle export tap

ROBOT VOICE. Apology Workshop

LOUIS. Click drag click drag toggle export taaaaap

ROBOT VOICE. Radical Compassion

LOUIS. *("Microphone echo.")* Compassion compassion compassion

>*(It's super goofy. But kind of sweet.)*

(Still on a "microphone.") And now! Everybody! Put your hands together! For the one! The only! DJ...

Tess!

TESS. Oh that is a terrible DJ name

>*(**TESS** and **LOUIS** laugh.)*

>*(**TESS** takes over.)*

>*(**LOUIS** does a silly back-up beat to her clicks.)*

(In a weird way, it helps. **TESS** *gets into a rhythm.)*

(A little while of this: the "music" of the intake process, punctuated by that robot voice.)

(They are efficient together.)

(Click click click.)

ROBOT VOICE. Drama Therapy

(Click drag click drag toggle export tap.)

Art Therapy

(Click drag click drag toggle export tap.)

Body Language Bingo

(Click drag click drag toggle export tap.)

Two-Week Extension

LOUIS. Daaaaaamn

TESS. Two more weeks motherfuckerrrrr

LOUIS. Hey you want something better than coffee?

TESS. How?

*(**LOUIS** opens up a cabinet.)*

(It's actually a fridge.)

(A six-pack appears.)

Whaaaaat

LOUIS. Left over from last week's happy hour

TESS. They are so good to us

LOUIS. Just brace yourself for the parties they throw here. The Halloween one gets, sloppy

TESS. Noted

(They each take a sip of beer.)

LOUIS. So are you a transplant?

TESS. How'd you guess

LOUIS. Your parking job

TESS. Oh no

LOUIS. Was

creative

TESS. Yeahhh I'm more of a train, bus person

LOUIS. Who suddenly got curious about freeways?

TESS. Needed a change

LOUIS. You like, on the lam?

TESS. *(Playing along.)* Nailed it

LOUIS. But really

(**TESS** *takes a sip of beer.)*

(Then:)

TESS. You ever work at a lab?

LOUIS. Nope

TESS. So much solitude. Like an alarming amount of solitude. Way too much time to just be inside my own brain. Which was [not good]

Sometimes, if I was feeling really loopy, I would – All right don't think I'm insane

LOUIS. I won't, promise

TESS. Sometimes I would

talk

to the mice

LOUIS. *(?)* You would

Talk to them

TESS. Yep. I got to a point where I was Talking to the mice

(Trying to downplay.) I wasn't doing like, a Mouse Voice back, but I would have some

brief

one-sided

chats

LOUIS. The Mice Whisperer

TESS. No uh uh that is not gonna be my new nickname

LOUIS. We'll see

TESS. I don't know, maybe I'm an idiot. It was a good job.

LOUIS. But was it?

TESS. Yeah, was it? In name. In name it was a good job. But it was either too lonely or too competitive. And for what? People were just trying to win genius grants and I came into this field because I want to help change the world – oh my god I just heard myself say, "I want to help change the world"

LOUIS. It's okay, you did win the science fair

TESS. (Twice)

I love the tidiness of this work, you know?

Because I really think everything has a logical solution, it's just that most people are too lazy to do the calculations. I really think it's possible to dump all your pain and your grief and your messy, whatever, into a beautifully constructed equation, like yes, please, thank you, and you guys are Doing That

LOUIS. Wow. You like, capital B believe in this place. Natalia must love you

TESS. She didn't exactly give off that impression...

LOUIS. That'll change once she learns you uprooted your whole life because you're obsessed with the algorithm

TESS. Yeah.

>   *(Wasn't going to reveal this, but...)*

Well I was also

living with my

boyfriend

And then we broke up. And I said, "It's fine, I'll move"

And I think he thought I meant like, to Queens but

LOUIS. *(!)* Ohhh but you meant /

TESS. Across the country. Yeah.

I don't really do drastic things like that normally. But, I was talking to mice and, I needed to get out of that city

LOUIS. I heard rent is nuts over there

TESS. Yeah. Yeah.

...and also

You ever live in a place that's just dripping in, memories of other people?

LOUIS. *(You lost me.)* Kinda

TESS. *(Whoops.)* Well. Anyway. I somehow charmed Dr. Quill on video chat, sold a bunch of my plasma and,

Here we are

LOUIS. Cheers newbie. Welcome.

>   *(Clink.)*
>
>   *(Drink.)*
>
>   *(They look at each other.)*

TESS. What

LOUIS. Nothing

TESS. You seem like you're Not Saying something

LOUIS. Oh are you one of those people? Who thinks everyone has this like, vast interior?

TESS. No I think most people are full of shit

LOUIS. Most people are just spacing out

> *(Darkness.)*

A VERY SOOTHING VOICE. Do you ever feel like you're on a hamster wheel? Wake up with a crick in your neck from your discount mattress, clock in, clock out, microwave some frozen pad thai, fall asleep to the grainy glow of a sitcom and then do it all over again? Have you ever wanted your life to have purpose? Look no further than The Gradient! Join our trailblazing staff of scientists, engineers, programmers and mathematicians, and play a crucial role in revolutionizing contrition and accountability across the globe! Competitive salary, medical, dental, vision, and stock options all included, plus complimentary food and beverage, daily wellness options, and a Fun and Lively work environment if we do say so ourselves! Ha ha ha!

(Rapidly.) Adaptability and efficiency is mandatory must be willing to think on your feet and handle highly sensitive material people with thin skins who aren't team players need not apply

3.

(Lights snap to **JACKSON** *in spotlight.)*

(The following scene takes place over the course of two weeks.)

(The space between **TESS** *and a client interaction could be an hour, or three days, or seven, etc.)*

(Time expands as **TESS** *gets to know The Gradient, and the clients progress through its programming.)*

JACKSON. I'm sorry

I'm really sorry. I had no idea. That you felt the way you felt, about what we [ ]

I didn't even Come Close to seeing it That Way, is the thing. Like my mind is *(Mind-blown sound/gesture.)*

So. Thank you? Thank you. For sharing your side of the – I'm grateful that you still want to

Talk to me

Look at me

I'm So Sorry.

If I could just like, I don't know – build you a tower of sorrys. If I could Bathe You in sorrys (maybe that sounds –)

If I could, cook you up a stir-fry of sorrys. A truly epic stir-fry – none of that, whatever-the-hell is in my fridge bullshit. It would be perfectly seasoned, with the most like, delicate sauce-to-food ratio And nothing soggy, nothing soggy at all. Just the right Crunch, just the right texture. So that you would be eating this, bountiful, flavorful

Garden of my sorrys. I wish I could /

A VOICE. I'm going to stop you right there

>   *(Lights shift.)*

>   *(The* **VOICE** *was* **TESS.***)*

>   *(She comes into view.)*

TESS. Okay. That was [ ]

> That was okay.

JACKSON. I was going off on a little bit of a tangent

TESS. You were, yeah

JACKSON. Maybe I should cut down on the metaphor

TESS. That's probably a good plan

JACKSON. Just tell me what's not working. I'd love to hear what's not working

>   *(***TESS** *looks at* **JACKSON.***)*

>   *(There's a lot that's not working.)*

TESS. How about we start with what Is working, because sometimes when you see That it can help / you –

JACKSON. Help you see what isn't working rightrightright. I totally get that

> Totally get that

>   *(***TESS** *isn't thrilled he keeps interrupting her. She consults her notes.)*

TESS. So. When you said you were grateful that she was talking to you and looking at you? That was nice. Acknowledging that is nice

JACKSON. Okay sweet

TESS. And there was a moment when you said: "I don't know" and that / was

JACKSON. Not ideal, of course. Gotta be precise, gotta be certain

TESS. We're actually still talking about what's working

JACKSON. Oh. So when I said "I don't know" that was

TESS. Working

JACKSON. *(?)* So it's a Good Thing to be inarticulate

TESS. It's important to be honest about not always having the answers, or the words

JACKSON. But I thought that's what I was avoiding

TESS. What

JACKSON. Not having the words

TESS. Well admitting what you don't know or understand is a key concept for you to hone going forward. That's called: Humility.

…

Do you want to write that down?

JACKSON. Nah. I've got it all *(Points to temple.)*

TESS. Ah. Audio learner over here

JACKSON. I actually have an, impeccable memory

TESS. Impeccable, okay

JACKSON. Like I remember that my first session with you, you were wearing green pants. And this v-neck shirt that showed a little more skin than you were comfortable with, because you kept smoothing your hair over your shoulder, trying to hide your collarbone, and cover up this pair of freckles you have *(Demonstrates.)* right here.

TESS. …

JACKSON. See? Crazy right? My memory.

(Instantly:)

*

CLIENT 1. *(Ivy League douche.)* I'm sorry. Okay?

I'm sorry.

TESS. ...Do you have anything else to add

CLIENT 1. *(A little exasperated.)* I'm sorry that – I'm sorry that you were offended

I'm sorry that you misinterpreted my actions

I'm sorry that you clearly don't have a sense of humor

I'm sorry that you overreacted.

TESS. All right. That was a [?]...nice jumping-off point. What I heard just now were a lot of "You" statements. Why don't you try again but this time, speak in "I" statements. So, for instance: I'm sorry that I behaved in a way that hurt you.

> **(CLIENT 1** *looks at* **TESS** *like she's an idiot.)*

..."I" statements, not "You" statements. Do you understand?

> **(CLIENT 1** *looks at* **TESS.** *Makes a very frustrated sigh.)*

CLIENT 1. Look, I went to Yale, okay?

*

TESS. Can you tell me about this object?

> **(TESS** *holds a small plant in her hands.)*

CLIENT 2. *(Surfer bro.)* Uhhh it's a plant

TESS. That's right. But today, I want you to think of this plant as if it were a person. A person you're on a date with

CLIENT 2. Uhhh okay, gotcha dude, gotcha

(**CLIENT 2** *approaches the plant as if it were a person he's on a date with.*)

TESS. So, is she enjoying your company? Is she having fun?

CLIENT 2. *(Truly stumped.)* I have no idea

TESS. And why is that?

CLIENT 2. Because a plant

can't

talk

TESS. Yes! You need verbal cues. And what's the opposite of a verbal cue

CLIENT 2. A

Non-verbal cue?

*

TESS. *(Re: the plant.)* How would you feel if this person were sitting across from you right now?

CLIENT 3. *(Tough dude.)* That's not a person, that's a plant

TESS. Right, but for the exercise

CLIENT 3. Why would I talk to, whatever the fuck type of plant this is

TESS. I think it's a / fern?

CLIENT 3. This is fucking stupid

TESS. *(Trying to salvage.)* Um – so in your Opinion, this exercise is not something you want to engage with?

CLIENT 3. *(Duh.)* Yeah, that's what I just said

TESS. Why don't you try using the word Opinion when you make a statement like that

CLIENT 3. "In my opinion" this "exercise" is fucking stupid

TESS. Okay. That was

better

CLIENT 3. Who the hell buys into this shit?

TESS. *(A pivot.)* ...You tell me. Who buys into this shit?

CLIENT 3. People with, like zero IQ. People I can't stand

TESS. And who can't you stand?

CLIENT 3. ...Dumb people

TESS. Who else?

CLIENT 3. Fake people

TESS. Who else?

CLIENT 3. Liars

TESS. Good! Who else? Who else?

*

> (**CLIENT 4** *is drawing intensely with crayons.*)

It looks like you're working on quite the masterpiece over there

> (**CLIENT 4** *keeps drawing. He's pressing down really hard with the crayons.*)

Just make sure you don't, rip the paper, haha!

> (**CLIENT 4** *puts the crayons down.*)

Do you want to

show me what you made?

> (**CLIENT 4** *displays his drawing.*)

> (*It's strange and unintelligible. Mainly just a collection of large, darkly-colored blobs and scribbles.*)

TESS. This is your self-portrait?

>   *(***CLIENT 4*** nods.)*

Okay

I

like what you did there

*

>   *(***CLIENT 5*** hands **TESS** the sketchpad.)*

CLIENT 5. *(Distinguished older gentleman.)* Here you are

>   *(***TESS** considers the drawing.)*

TESS. So I'm seeing a sad face, surrounded by a lot of question marks. Is that right?

CLIENT 5. That's correct

TESS. So I'm getting the sense that the future looks a little bleak to you, and also confusing

CLIENT 5. Well in the future I see myself getting smaller and smaller. And more bewildered

TESS. Okay, by what?

CLIENT 5. By how I'm supposed to comport myself. By all these new, Cultural Norms. There's no Respect anymore for the elders, for our wisdom and our sense of humor

TESS. But don't you think there's room for / new

CLIENT 5. There is No Respect

*

TESS. So you've done mask work before?

CLIENT 6. *(Mr. Nice Guy.)* OH yeah. I'm a classically trained actor so, mask work, clown work, improv, Shakespeare, I've Done It All

TESS. *(...)* That's

amazing

CLIENT 6. I've actually been in a few commercials? T-Mobile? State Farm? Maybe you recognize my [face]?

TESS. *(A lie.)* You do

look familiar

CLIENT 6. That's probably why, yeah. I am No Stranger to the spotlight, haha!

TESS. Great! I'm loving the enthusiasm. But to be clear: this isn't a performance. It's just a tool to access your subconscious.

CLIENT 6. Cool cool cool cool cool, yeah, got it

> *(**CLIENT 6** loosens up.)*
>
> *(Does he do some vocal warm-ups? A few stretches?)*
>
> *(**TESS** is kind of weirded out.)*

TESS. Um, okay. So now, when you put on the mask, I want you to embody how you believe other people view you. Whenever you're ready...

> *(**CLIENT 6** puts on the mask.)*
>
> *(He does a weird, very involved, very over-the-top performance. As if he's auditioning for Juilliard. Or something.)*
>
> *(He takes off the mask.)*

CLIENT 6. Wow. I really, REALLY felt that! You know sometimes when you're performing and you're just like, In It? I was so, so In It!

*

> *(**CLIENT 7** wears the mask.)*

TESS. Okay: You just asked a woman out, and she said no. And you really really liked her, and you found her really attractive. But she said no. Show me how you respond to that.

> (**CLIENT 7** *responds.*)

Good, good. Now: The same woman said no to you, but she didn't just say no to you privately, she rejected you publicly. In front of a lot of your friends

> (**CLIENT 7** *responds. Maybe crumples into a ball?*)

Great! Now: This woman is not only turning you down in front of your friends, she's also telling you that you're a bad person. She's saying over and over again, "You're a bad person." And how does that make you feel, when she says that? Show me how that makes you feel

You're a bad person

You're a bad person

You're a bad person

> (**CLIENT 7** *rips off the mask. He's kind of freaking out.*)

CLIENT 7. But I don't want to be! I don't want to be!

TESS. It's okay it's okay, you're okay

CLIENT 7. *(Breath.) (Breath.) (Breath.)*

TESS. I really, really feel like we're getting somewhere

CLIENT 7. Can we please *(Breath.)* take *(Breath.)* a break!

> *

TESS. Tell me about this image

> (*A loud click.*)

CLIENT 8. *(Gum-chewing.)* It's some girl

TESS. Some girl or some...

CLIENT 8. Woman. Right right. "Woman"

TESS. And what else can you tell me

CLIENT 8. She's smiling

TESS. So that means...

CLIENT 8. That she's happy? That's she's having a good time?

TESS. Yes, good, yes! Anything else to add?

CLIENT 8. She looks annoying

TESS. *(Uh-oh...)* She looks Annoying

CLIENT 8. Yeah she kinda looks like she has an irritating laugh

TESS. Okay...

CLIENT 8. She kinda looks like my ex

TESS. How

so

CLIENT 8. Because she looks like a bitch

TESS. *(Ugh...)* She looks like /

CLIENT 8. She looks like a bitch.

*

TESS. And what about this?

(A loud click.)

JACKSON. That is a girl crying

TESS. Great. And this?

(A loud click.)

JACKSON. That is also a girl [crying] –

Oh wait, that's a woman, that's a woman crying

TESS. Are you sure?

JACKSON. *(?)* That it's / a

TESS. That she's crying

JACKSON. Well I don't see tears, but it's clear that she's upset

TESS. Great. How do you know that?

JACKSON. You can tell from her shoulders, the way she's holding her shoulders

TESS. Say more

JACKSON. And her lip, there's a, there's a, what's the word

A quivering. Her lip is like mid-quiver

TESS. Good, very good. Anything else?

JACKSON. And she's not looking at the camera she's looking, off to the side, like she's – trying to get out of the frame. Like she doesn't want to be photographed at all

TESS. Exactly.

> *(A loud click.)*

Tell me about this image

JACKSON. That's someone being cat-called

> *(A loud click.)*

That's a frat party and a, woman who seems like she wants to leave the frat party

> *(A loud click.)*

That's the face of a person who doesn't want to be kissed on the neck

> *(A loud click.)*

And that's the face of a person who doesn't want to be grabbed by the arm

(A loud click.)

Or tossed on the bed

(A loud click.)

Or gripped by the hair

I feel like I'm on a roll here

(A loud click.)

(A loud click.)

TESS. Let me /

(A loud click.)

(A completion sound.)

Oh. It looks like that was the last image

Well done. You actually did great

JACKSON. "Actually"? You sound surprised

TESS. *(A revision.)* You did great.

JACKSON. So what's my score? On the algorithm.

TESS. That doesn't concern you

JACKSON. Doesn't it directly concern me?

TESS. Just focus on the new skills you're gaining and the algorithm will take care of itself

JACKSON. Come on, don't you want to get your commission?

TESS. This isn't a store

JACKSON. But if your clients do well, I'm guessing *you* do well

TESS. If my clients are rehabilitated, then *everyone* does well

JACKSON. Excellent marketing around here

TESS. It's more than marketing

JACKSON. I mean, I get it. PR makes or breaks your ROI. I'm the CEO of a start-up. Not sure I mentioned / [?]

TESS. It's in your file

JACKSON. Of course, my file. So you probably know my app's going live soon?

TESS. That's somewhere in your file too

JACKSON. By this time next year, we'll be experiencing widespread use, widespread membership. By this time next year, I'll have made it

TESS. ...Made the app

JACKSON. No the app has already been made. I'm talking like Making It. Like I will have Made It. Been successful. One and a half years tops, and I really feel like I'll have reached my first of multiple professional peaks.

TESS. That's

[   ]

impressive

JACKSON. Well you've got to send the universe whatever you want it to send back to you, you know?

TESS. ...Actually I don't

JACKSON. No?

TESS. I'm pretty superstitious

JACKSON. And self-deprecating?

TESS. Uh

JACKSON. It's all good. I think self-deprecation is super cute

(Weird beat.)

Sorry. That was probably – sorry

Wow it's kind of incredible: how good I've gotten at saying sorry

TESS. ...

JACKSON. Do you

disagree? Or –

TESS. *(Brushing off.)* What? No, it's great. Great progress

JACKSON. *(Unconvinced.)* Okay

TESS. ...

How do you know that

JACKSON. Know what?

TESS. That you're good at saying sorry

JACKSON. Well it's second-nature now. It's like, embedded in me these days

TESS. So that makes you good at it? If you say it all the time?

JACKSON. *(?)* Are we doing an exercise

TESS. Sort of. I'm just –

I'm not sure that saying sorry is the same as Feeling sorry

JACKSON. Can't have one without the other, right?

TESS. *(No.)* I don't –

But then what

JACKSON. Then – what?

TESS. How does your apology actually affect the people you've harmed? How does it impact your day-to-day life?

JACKSON. Isn't this all a little Personal?

TESS. You're supposed to get personal

JACKSON. I thought I was supposed to "gain new skills"

TESS. You can't fully internalize those skills unless you apply them

JACKSON. Is that what The Gradient thinks or what you think?

TESS. *(A lie.)* Both

JACKSON. *(Unconvinced.)* Uh-huh

Okay, okay, let's get personal then. What's your name?

TESS. *(?)* What?

JACKSON. Let's talk like, human to human for five seconds. Personal, right? What's your name?

TESS. It's against our standards of conduct to discuss that

JACKSON. That seems unreasonable

TESS. Why do you care so much

JACKSON. *(Simply.)* Because. I like you.

TESS. *(Psh.)* You don't know me

JACKSON. But I'm starting to. I know you're the smartest person here. That your brain moves so fast you're always ten steps ahead. That you work really fucking hard. Constantly questioning, and analyzing, while all the losers around you are just like, sleepwalking through the motions. Or picking dandruff out of their hair.

(**TESS** *is sort of charmed by this. Tries to hide it.*)

Plus it seems only natural, as we continue working together.

What's your name?

…

TESS. Tess. It's Tess.

(Darkness.)

A VERY SOOTHING VOICE. Would you like to hear some feedback from our clients?

"The Gradient has turned me into someone who is introspective and emotive. It has reacquainted me with a softer self." – Leonard P., Columbus, Ohio.

"The Gradient opened my eyes to my own flaws and carved out a way to mend them." – Andrew S., Brooklyn, New York.

"The Gradient is the best thing that ever happened to me. Period." – Kevin J., Palo Alto, California.

"The Gradient has taught me that I know how to make people smile. And crack up. And beam. That I know how to make people feel seen. And feel special." – Luke M., Nashville, Tennessee.

Thanks for sharing everyone. Food for thought, here at: The Gradient.

4.

(One week later.)

(Very, very early in the morning.)

*(**TESS** is doing intake.)*

(She's focused. Working speedily.)

(And then.)

*(**NATALIA** enters.)*

*(And **TESS** jumps.)*

NATALIA. *(?)* What are you doing here

TESS. I'm

trying to stay on top of my data entry. Plus we have that morning meeting

NATALIA. *(...)* In three hours

TESS. True. But at this point I thought I would just

Ride it out

NATALIA. Bad roommates?

TESS. What

NATALIA. Bad relationship?

TESS. Uh

NATALIA. Usually when people spend the night they don't want to go home

TESS. *(Realizing.)* Were you in session?

NATALIA. No. Going to sunrise yoga later. Want to make sure I snag a mat

TESS. Nice.

NATALIA. I'm kidding. Yes I was in session

TESS. This early?

NATALIA. I was on call

TESS. I didn't realize You had to be on call

NATALIA. Well sometimes employees flake

TESS. Uh-oh

NATALIA. It's fine. I can run on three hours

TESS. *(?)* Of

NATALIA. Sleep

TESS. Woah

NATALIA. Yeah it's a skill

> (**NATALIA** *begins opening a series of cabinets and drawers.*)
>
> (*And then slamming them shut. Loudly.*)
>
> (*She's looking for something.*)

(Where the hell –)

> (*Slam.*)

(Cheap ass –)

> (*Slam*)
>
> (*Slam.*)

TESS. You okay?

> (**NATALIA** *continues opening and closing cabinets.*)

NATALIA. I'm fine

> (*Slam.*)

There's just Nothing To Eat in this place

TESS. I could send an email to Maureen. To let her know supply's low

NATALIA. She knows.

Here we go!

> (**NATALIA** *pulls out a box of granola bars.*)

> (*But the box is empty.*)

GOD [dammit]

> (**NATALIA** *crushes the empty box.*)

> (**TESS** *looks at her.*)

> (*Looks away.*)

TESS. There's some string cheese in the fridge

> (**NATALIA** *considers. Opens the fridge.*)

> (*Takes out a string cheese. Bites into it.*)

You really just, go for it

> (**NATALIA** *finishes the string cheese.*)

NATALIA. What *is* that? What is that part of your brain that thinks food will, Fuel You

TESS. ...Well it does. Fuel you

NATALIA. *(Snaps.)* Yes I know. I realize it literally fuels us

TESS. Sorry /

NATALIA. But there are so many times when I think I'll eat something and then, bam: back on track. I'm a person again. Oh you're pissed off? You're actually just hungry. Oh you're down? You're hungry. And then I'm inhaling four servings of ravioli and I feel exactly the same You should forget this conversation. This is unprofessional you should forget this conversation

TESS. …Understood

> (**TESS** *goes back to working.*)

> (**NATALIA** *stands there, crumpling her string cheese wrappers into little balls. Something's clearly up.*)

> (*She can't help herself.*)

NATALIA. We used to date

TESS. You and

Louis?

NATALIA. What?

TESS. *(…)* What?

NATALIA. Me and #6221. The guy I / just

TESS. Oh! Oh my god. The guy you / just

NATALIA. Did intake for. Yeah

TESS. Shouldn't they have some kind of system in place? To prevent that from happening?

NATALIA. That's a privacy breach. You can't be required to document your whole romantic history. I mean What Are The Chances. It's crazy. It's insane. It's funny it's really funny

TESS. It's okay if it's not

funny

NATALIA. But it Is funny. That's what I just said, It's funny.

TESS. Okay.

> (**TESS** *gets back to work.*)

> (*And then:*)

NATALIA. He has

So many more moles than I remembered. He's just like

Covered

in moles

TESS. Hope he's getting

checked

NATALIA. *(?)* What

TESS. Like, you know, skin cancer. Checked

NATALIA. Oh right sure

(**NATALIA** *is elsewhere.*)

It's bizarre to think there was a time in my life when I actually wanted him to die

TESS. *(...)* Of skin cancer

NATALIA. Of anything. There was a time in my life when I was so like, dizzy with rage that I wished death on him. Some, medieval death. I would picture him covered in boils. His gums falling out

TESS. I used to fantasize about running over my ex's face whenever I was on a treadmill

NATALIA. That's [   ]

TESS. Forced me to run faster

NATALIA. Sure

TESS. Did he seem

different

NATALIA. No he was exactly the same.

TESS. Well joke's on him. I bet he was really intimidated. I bet he was like, "shaking in his boots." Staring at the co-founder of a major institution

NATALIA. He seemed bored. And indignant. Mainly bored

TESS. That'll change once The Gradient gets through to him. Right?

NATALIA. *(Unconvinced...)* Of course. Right.

> *(**NATALIA** is elsewhere.)*
>
> *(**TESS** works.)*
>
> *(And then decides to:)*

TESS. It must have been,

really intense. If I had to be in the same room as one of my past, you know – I'd, lose my stomach, my balance, lose a lot of things. Because there are always those People who stay imprinted on your – not heart. Oh god Not Heart that sounds [ridiculous]. They're just lodged in there, somewhere. Festering. And it's like: Really? Really? You Still matter? You Still affect me? Can you leave me alone please can you leave my brain please can you

NATALIA. Yeah... It's not quite like that. For me

TESS. Oh

NATALIA. Not quite that extreme

TESS. Oh. Of course

NATALIA. See you at the morning meeting.

TESS. Yeah. See you at the /

> *(Lights shift onto **NATALIA**.)*
>
> *(The morning meeting.)*
>
> *(Her tone is decidedly more business.)*

NATALIA. Okay people hello hello, morning meeting. Thanks for being on time. Remember, early means on time, on time means late. Late means don't even bother coming. But, preaching to the choir here –

I see your hand Doug, I see it and I'm gonna get to you at the end okay?

All right, some news: unfortunately, there was a miscommunication with our food distributor this week. So our snack supply has been cut in half until further notice

(Groans.)

Yes, I know. It's not ideal. So let's just all collectively agree to not be assholes about it. Which means don't take five granola bars, take two. And also: if the coffee's out, make another pot. If the machine's busted, tell someone. Not me, that is 100 percent not my job. Talk to an intern. Like Sandra.

Xandra. Sorry, I'll get that – I promise you one day I'll get that

LOUIS. ...It's their last day

NATALIA. Wow time flies

I see your hand Doug can we,

Thanks

Everyone: please continue to review the conduct manual on Language. That's old staff as well as new. Never hurts to brush up. When you are in session you are representing The Gradient and speaking on behalf of The Gradient and its tenets. Remember: be BARE. Can we just – Humor me, can we –

(The "crowd" says the acronym. In clumsy unison.)

(With the crowd.) B – Breezy

A – Authoritative

R – Rigorous

E – Ethical

>   (**TESS** *raises her hand.*)

I said questions at the end, Tess

TESS. What if my question's about the acronym

NATALIA. Fine, what

TESS. Are we prioritizing being breezy or being authoritative

NATALIA. Both

TESS. Okay. Could I get some clarity on Breezy

NATALIA. *(?)* Sunny, Airy, Brisk

LOUIS. It means keep things light

NATALIA. You keep things light, they tell you their inner monologue. You make them feel attacked, they clam up. But also be direct and in charge. Yin and yang. This is how we get the algorithm to work its magic. *(Earnest question.)* Did you miss this part of training?

TESS. No no I'm trained I'm good

>   (**NATALIA** *isn't quite convinced about that.*)
>
>   (*She returns to her notes.*)

NATALIA. Let's see… Community building, great, we're a team, great, don't talk to the media. Yeah, don't talk to the media unless you've been media trained. That's important. Seriously.

(Consults notes.) What else what else. Oh: the R&D team has uploaded a one-pager about a new program The Gradient will be launching soon. Please give it a read directly after this meeting.

And Riley's sick today

>   (*Groans.*)

NATALIA. So if your client loads are larger, you can thank her.

Doug you had a / [question?]

> *(Post-meeting,* LOUIS *and* TESS *consult the one-pager.)*

LOUIS. It's called the Fast Track

TESS. Like, Disney World?

LOUIS. That's Fast Pass

TESS. Oh right

LOUIS. Different enough that we can't get sued

TESS. *(Reading.)* If a client scores above-average in three or more of the algorithm's categories, they get rewarded with a shortened Gradient stay

LOUIS. Isn't it wild?

TESS. Yeah that's absurd

LOUIS. *(Different wavelength.)* Wait what? You know I'm on R&D, right?

TESS. Sorry. Not trying to undermine your work

LOUIS. Don't sweat it. It's not my baby. But it is kind of brilliant

TESS. High praise

LOUIS. No more wasting resources on the clients who are killing it so we can spend necessary resources on the clients who aren't

TESS. How do you define clients, killing it

LOUIS. It's all numbers-based, don't worry. We're piloting this whole plug-in for the algorithm.

TESS. When is it being implemented?

LOUIS. Friday

TESS. Shouldn't it be, vetted a little bit first?

LOUIS. *(Jokey.)* Wow, Super Fan is really down on the R&D team today

TESS. No no, it's just – isn't shortening clients' stays sort of, at odds with this entire operation…

LOUIS. Or maybe it's proving that the operation is working efficiently

TESS. How short of a stay would / they

LOUIS. Hey don't you have sessions right now?

TESS. Oh shit

LOUIS. Mid-term check-ins?

TESS. Exactly

LOUIS. You got this! Knock 'em / [dead!]

> *(Lights snap to Room Four.)*
>
> *(Everyone vanishes except* **TESS** *and* **CLIENT 4***. It's like a Less Shitty Dude Ballet.)*
>
> *(***CLIENT 4** *is nodding.)*

TESS. Yes, you've learned a lot so far?

> *(***CLIENT 4** *nods.)*

And how about growth, have you sensed any growth over the past three weeks?

> *(***CLIENT 4** *does nothing.)*

Okay. Got it.

CLIENT 4. In my opinion, yes

TESS. *(?)* Oh my god you talk

CLIENT 4. …Did you think I didn't know how

TESS. You just haven't spoken a word during any of our sessions

CLIENT 4. Well there you go. Growth

*

CLIENT 1. I'm an on-the-go guy, you know? I don't always take time to, Reflect. But here it's like, reflecting on steroids

TESS. And have you discovered anything during these periods of reflection?

CLIENT 1. That, I don't always have to lecture people. Or interrupt them. Or

TESS. Is that – did you have more to say?

CLIENT 1. I'm just – trying not to interrupt you

TESS. Oh

Thank – you

*

CLIENT 5. And lately I've come to terms with the fact that: This is a different time. This is a different generation

TESS. *(This again?)* Different how

*

CLIENT 2. *(Surfer bro.)* Consent dude, I never really got it! Like I got it but I didn't Get It

TESS. Until you came here?

CLIENT 2. Yah

TESS. Okay, that's

progress

*

CLIENT 6. *(Mr. Nice Guy.)* I overcompensate, I see that now! I overcompensate. I put on an act! I fuck with people

TESS. In what way

CLIENT 6. Like I pretend that I'm interested in what they're saying to me, when I'm really not

*

TESS. Breathe, remember? Breatheeee

(**CLIENT 7** *breathes.*)

CLIENT 7. I don't want people to hate me

TESS. And what did we say about that?

CLIENT 7. That it's

out of my control

TESS. But what can you control?

CLIENT 7. My actions. My behavior

TESS. Right, right

*

CLIENT 3. *(Tough dude.)* I've realized that I'm basically a fucking coward most of the time

TESS. What would you say you're afraid of?

CLIENT 3. That people will think I'm a hack. That people will think I'm unattractive. That I'll get passed over. That everything I do or say will be misinterpreted. Or seen as evil. That I actually am evil. That I'll be forgotten. That my career will implode. That I have no real purpose

*

CLIENT 8. *(Gum chewing.)* I think I hate women

TESS. You – [?]

CLIENT 8. That's my main takeaway, from being here

(Gum chew.)

(Gum chew.)

(Gum chew.)

I think I hate women

*

TESS. Do you feel guilt about what you've done?

CLIENT 1. You could call it that

*

TESS. Do you feel guilt about what you've done?

CLIENT 2. Yeahhhhh

*

TESS. Do you feel guilt about what you've done?

CLIENT 3. Uh-huh

*

CLIENT 4. Yep

*

CLIENT 5. Yes ma'am

*

CLIENT 6. Absolutely

*

CLIENT 7. *(Hyperventilating and nodding.)*

*

CLIENT 8. Kinda?

*

TESS. *(With power.)* Do you feel guilt about what you've done?

JACKSON. Yes. I do.

> *(Lights snap.)*
>
> *(We're back to a room with* JACKSON *and* TESS.*)*

TESS. And what specifically do you feel guilty for?

JACKSON. Do we really have to get into that

TESS. It's a simple question

JACKSON. But I said yes, I feel guilty, isn't that what you want?

TESS. It isn't about what I want

JACKSON. Can we just

move on

TESS. You're doing it again. You're backing away when things get [   ]

JACKSON. When things get what

TESS. That's what I'm trying to figure out. What you're scared to face

JACKSON. *(Psh.)* I'm not scared to face anything

TESS. Say that again

JACKSON. *(Sort of convincing.)* I'm not scared to face anything

TESS. Again

JACKSON. *(Less convincing.)* I'm not

scared to face anything

TESS. Again

JACKSON. I can't stop thinking about this Expression, on her face. On the night that we were, you know, the Night in Question, the night that we were [   ]. Maybe expression is the wrong [word]

TESS. It's okay. Keep going

JACKSON. She was blank. Not like, deer in headlights but, checked out. Physically there but Mentally, hovering above herself. Like she was trying to will herself elsewhere. Somewhere warm maybe – a beach, Japan, I don't know. Somewhere far away from me.

TESS. And do you think that's happened before

JACKSON. Yeah. Yeah. So Many women I've been with have had that expression on their faces – or that, non-expression, while we were [having sex]. Like Shelley. My college [girlfriend], you know when I was in college, Shelley was my –

I want to reach out. I'm gonna reach out. To her. But could we – could I practice? On you?

TESS. Not on a, photo or / a

JACKSON. No I think it would really help me if I practiced on /

(Another light shift.)

(An apology role-play.)

*(**TESS** toggles between **SHELLEY** and herself.)*

Hey Shelley.

SHELLEY. Hey.

JACKSON. How are you?

SHELLEY. I'm

doing well. Doing well.

JACKSON. I'm

so relieved to hear that

TESS. Don't say you're relieved

JACKSON. Why? I want her to be doing well

TESS. Just remember she's doing well *in spite* of you – your actions still affected her

JACKSON. Okay, sure, but

TESS. Keep going

JACKSON. Shelley, do you remember when we were dating?

SHELLEY. Yes

JACKSON. And do you remember how, when we were dating, I didn't always uh. Well I didn't always consider what you –

TESS. Just say it plainly

JACKSON. Do you remember those nights when we had sex

and I didn't care that I was hurting you? And it was consensual, technically –

SHELLEY. Technically

JACKSON. But I wanted it way way more than you did

SHELLEY. And I was pretty much just a body in space to you

JACKSON. So you remember?

SHELLEY. Yes

JACKSON. Like all-the-time remember or once-in-a-while remember?

SHELLEY. All the time

JACKSON. Oh god do you really think she'd say that

TESS. I do

JACKSON. I bet she's moved on

TESS. I bet those memories follow her around whenever she has sex now

JACKSON. No, no I bet she's moved on

TESS. Easier said than done

JACKSON. So what will she say?

TESS. She'll say: Yeah. I remember. She'll say: You were the person who taught me that sex was about steeling myself. Lying there and waiting it out, while you did whatever you wanted. And I was, basically a receptacle

JACKSON. Come on, a receptacle?

TESS. I was beside the point

JACKSON. I was a kid

TESS. Don't make excuses

JACKSON. I was a horny, drunken kid

TESS. More excuses

JACKSON. It's not an excuse if it's true

TESS. Take responsibility

JACKSON. I do, I do take responsibility

TESS. Okay so

JACKSON. I can take responsibility and also acknowledge that I was stupid and young

TESS. So then you don't take responsibility

JACKSON. But I can't believe / that I

TESS. You "can't believe"?

JACKSON. No I don't mean, fuck – that's the wrong [phrasing]

TESS. Don't waste time hedging this. Don't deny

JACKSON. I'm not denying / I'm

TESS. Accept it. Hear me and believe me and accept it

JACKSON. Okay. Okay. Okay. I accept it. I believe you. Because it really happened

TESS. What did

JACKSON. I hurt you, I made you feel terrible, it happened. And I'm gonna hold onto that for a long long long time, as a constant reminder. To be better. Because that's what you deserved

TESS. What

JACKSON. Better

TESS. …

JACKSON. You don't have to forgive me. I can always be the asshole who objectified you, who treated you with such, disregard. But still

I'm sorry, Shelley. I'm so, so sorry

I'm sorry and I'm guilty and I'm growing

> *(A moment.)*
>
> *(And then:)*
>
> (**JACKSON** *gulps down a glass of water, quickly.)*
>
> *(Almost as if nothing out of the ordinary has happened at all.)*

Wow

That. Felt. Amazing! It's honestly like a weight has been lifted! Like a physical weight has been lifted from my shoulders. Or maybe my ribs. Or maybe my, my jaw? It's like I've been holding all this tension in my jaw and now – damn. Do you see this? Do you see how loose and light I am right now?

TESS. *(Not at all feeling loose and light.)* I

    Yeah, I do

JACKSON. Thanks Tess, you're the best. You're my favorite. You know that? You're my favorite.

       *(*JACKSON *winks.)*

       (Darkness.)

A VERY SOOTHING VOICE. Are you looking for a way to give back? How would you like to become an agent for change? While most of our clients make the honorable decision to personally fund their stays here, The Gradient is always seeking investors and donations. Just $1 a day could help ten clients learn how to say they're sorry. We accept all major credit cards and Bitcoin.

5.

(Lights snap.)

(Natalia's office.)

(A day or so later.)

NATALIA. You wanted to discuss something?

TESS. In confidence, if that's possible.

NATALIA. In confidence, of course

TESS. I was wondering if I could inquire about the status of one of my clients. #5247

> *(**NATALIA** consults a chart.)*

NATALIA. Jackson Cuthbert, tech CEO

TESS. That's the one

> *(**NATALIA** consults a chart. Then:)*

NATALIA. He's been Fast Tracked

TESS. He's been Fast Tracked?

NATALIA. Correct. Introspection and externalized guilt scores were particularly strong.

TESS. …

  I don't buy it

NATALIA. You don't buy what?

TESS. His score

NATALIA. Are you recommending a revision?

TESS. *(!)* Oh can I do that?

NATALIA. It's highly involved. And usually only conducted by very senior employees

TESS. Well. I'm willing to risk it

NATALIA. What's your take

TESS. I'm

suspicious of how much he's progressing versus how much he's just, performing. I found his demeanor at intake to be quite different from his demeanor more recently

NATALIA. That's literally exactly what we're looking for. Growth

TESS. Is it growth? Or is it just that he's learned how to read the room?

NATALIA. It's increased emotional intelligence

TESS. Knowing the right things to say is not necessarily /

NATALIA. Developing new language is a concrete gain

TESS. Are employees ever a part of the algorithm's decision making?

NATALIA. What do you mean? All the data is human-generated. You can't get a number on the empathy scale by talking to a screen. That's why you're here

TESS. Right, of course. But – are there any plans to expand the algorithm?

NATALIA. It took two years to build, what exactly are you suggesting we expand?

TESS. I just wish we tested for authenticity

NATALIA. *(A joke.)* Do you want to hook clients up to lie detectors?

TESS. *(Not joking.)* Maybe?

NATALIA. That sounds wasteful and unproductive.

TESS. I thought we were supposed to be innovating. That's – what you told me day one

NATALIA. We encourage innovation within the bounds of our methodology, not outside of them

TESS. Doesn't really sound like innovation then

NATALIA. Doesn't really sound like you've ever run a major organization made up of trustees, shareholders, donors, management, and staff all with competing interests that you're asked to balance. Does it?

(A breath.)

TESS. What is Jackson's assignment, after he leaves here?

NATALIA. *(?)* His assignment

TESS. Yeah, I know that clients leave to become domestic violence hotline volunteers, or to mentor ninth-graders about consent. So, what's his next step?

*(***NATALIA*** *sighs.)*

NATALIA. Those partnerships are extremely rare

TESS. *(?)* I thought they were a central component of The Gradient's process. In any interviews you / give

NATALIA. We mention the few clients who've engaged with that type of work. Nowhere do we claim that that's the norm

TESS. Shouldn't it be the norm

NATALIA. Do you know how hard it is to try to convince a school principal that a man who used to recklessly send dick pics should be mentoring her students?

(A moment.)

*(Then ***TESS*** tries to stick her landing.)*

TESS. I think Jackson is bluffing. I think a lot of these people are bluffing. And the only thing they learn here is how to rig the system. How to go through the motions and check all the boxes and then leave. And when they get out, this whole experience will feel like a minor inconvenience. It doesn't cost them anything.

NATALIA. So

TESS. *(?)* So?

NATALIA. If they get another allegation, they come back

TESS. They come *back*?

NATALIA. Don't act shocked. That's always been an option

TESS. *(!)* And then the cycle repeats?

NATALIA. *(Correction.)* And then the rest of the world is down one asshole for six weeks, I will take that small victory

TESS. (Miniscule victory)

NATALIA. We are a well-oiled machine at this point. So unless you want to make yourself miserable, I'd recommend being a cog, okay? It's not sexy but you'll stay sane. And if feeling Virtuous or Important is that much of a priority for you well then you should probably say a little mantra to yourself in the morning about how you're making a teeny tiny dent in a massively impaired culture. And maybe someday that dent will grow a little bigger and a little bigger and then crack open and reveal the divine feminine spirit or whatever the fuck and heal the wounds and reverse the paradigm and end all the harm forever and into infinity but until then, we're just making dents. If you squint.

TESS. I don't want to squint

NATALIA. It's hard, isn't it

TESS. *(Thinks they're on the same page.)* God, yes

NATALIA. *(They're not.)* I mean when you have high expectations. Dream job, right? I try to enter most situations with the lowest expectations possible, so I'm never disappointed

TESS. I'm not disappointed / I'm

NATALIA. But you are. What do you want? To lock them up? Torture them? Abuse them back?

> (**NATALIA** *stares at* **TESS.**)
>
> *(Waits.)*

TESS. I'd like to request a transfer.

NATALIA. To a different department?

TESS. A client transfer. Jackson Cuthbert

NATALIA. What exactly would we be filing under this transfer?

TESS. I find that the, tenor of our sessions can sometimes become

inappropriate

NATALIA. Inappropriate how

TESS. He's, not very conscientious of boundaries

NATALIA. Of course he's not. That's why he's here

TESS. I realize that but /

NATALIA. *You* set the boundaries. I told you this day one. You Create The Boundaries

TESS. He's, pried into my personal life. He's spoken to me as if I were an ex-girlfriend, he's

He makes me uncomfortable

> *(A moment.)*

NATALIA. Does he ever make physical contact?

TESS. No

NATALIA. Crude gestures?

TESS. I don't think so, no

NATALIA. Has he propositioned you?

TESS. No

NATALIA. Threatened you?

TESS. No

NATALIA. Do you feel like you're in danger?

TESS. That's such a charged word

NATALIA. It's an important word

TESS. *(Suddenly remembering.)* He winked at me

NATALIA. He winked at you

TESS. You asked if there were any, crude gestures and at the end of our last session, he winked at me.

NATALIA. You would call that a

crude

gesture

TESS. Well, in context

NATALIA. Just to make sure I fully understand: Is there any part of you that also feels good?

TESS. *(?)* What

NATALIA. When he treats you this way.

TESS. I'm confused

NATALIA. You can say no. I asked you a question

TESS. So then no

NATALIA. No, what?

TESS. No it doesn't make me feel good it makes me feel uncomfortable that's / why I

NATALIA. All the time? Most of the time? Half the time? And the other half, against your better judgment you, sort of like it? And then hate yourself for liking it? But still, there it is: You liking it.

*(***NATALIA** *looks at her notes.)*

Well. Think on that. But I'm sorry to inform you, I cannot honor your request

TESS. Why?

NATALIA. Do you want me to transfer you every time you're paired with someone who sucks? Do you realize where you work? You'd be out of a job "He winked at me." I mean seriously, I have way bigger things to deal with right now: Ass grabs. Stalkers. Employees who have been Attacked. If you'll excuse me

(Darkness.)

A VERY SOOTHING VOICE. Listen: We know that here at The Gradient, we spend a lot of time critiquing behavior and demanding change. But we also know that gratitude is a virtue. And what is The Gradient grateful for? You. That's right. You. Our clients. Thank you for your eagerness to reach your real potential. Thank you for your desire to transform and redeem. And above all, thank you, from the bottom of our hearts, for not being rapists. A round of applause, for our clients, for not being rapists.

(The audience applauds. Or if they don't, the previous line must be repeated until they do.)

(Really, until they do.)

Thank you. Thank you so much. We just wanted to offer you a small token of our appreciation.

6.

(Loud music.*)

*(***NATALIA*** *in spotlight.)*

(She is dancing her face off.)

(She is kind of spectacular.)

(And she is in costume.)

(Because it's The Gradient Halloween party.)

(A moment of this and then:)

(Lights shift.)

(We no longer see ***NATALIA.****)*

(But we do see ***TESS*** *and* ***LOUIS.*** *Also in costume.)*

(And a little drunk.)

TESS. This *is* sloppy

LOUIS. The punch is toxic

TESS. I feel like I'm twenty-two again

LOUIS. Think that's the point

TESS. Was Natalia *dancing*?

LOUIS. You missed that??

TESS. No I didn't miss it I just wanted to Confirm like I need Confirmation. It was Natalia, *dancing*?

LOUIS. It was Natalia Breaking it Down

TESS. Did not see that coming from her

---

*A license to produce *The Gradient* does not include a performance license for any third-party or copyrighted music. Licensees should create an original composition or use music in the public domain. For further information, please see the Music and Third-Party Materials Use Note on page iii.

LOUIS. What, you have better moves?

TESS. I have some amazing moves

LOUIS. Wouldn't expect that, Science Fair

TESS. God I'm starving, are you starving

LOUIS. Maybe you should scope out the leftovers from the Silicon Valley bros

TESS. I already did. They ordered Thai but by the time I got there all that was left was beansprouts

LOUIS. Oh, damn

TESS. *(Ugh.)* My body is like eighty-percent Tequila right now

LOUIS. Same

TESS. Remember when Halloween was about candy

LOUIS. No truly no recollection

TESS. When was the last time you went trick-or-treating?

LOUIS. ...Fifth grade.

TESS. *(!)* That's early

LOUIS. That was my best costume: Grapes

TESS. Purple balloons?

LOUIS. *(A little proud?)* Yep

TESS. It was seventh grade for me. Or wait – sixth. In seventh grade I thought we were trick-or-treating but we ended up running around the woods and playing truth or dare

LOUIS. Aww did you bring your pillowcase and everything?

TESS. I think I actually did! It was me and Katie S. and Katie M. and a bunch of guys I didn't really talk to *(Remembering.)* and Nika DiPaolo!

LOUIS. *(Playing along.)* Love Nika, great girl

TESS. *(Remembering.)* And one of the dares was that Nika would flash the guys. I remember her like, perched underneath this huge tree, her back to me and the Katies, the guys waiting in front of her with a flashlight. And then I remember hearing *(Middle-school boy voice.)* "oh yeahhh" "yessss" "there we gooo"

LOUIS. *(Laughing.)* Classic

TESS. And I was standing there pretending to judge her, but

[I wasn't]

Oh that's probably the first time I [   ]

LOUIS. What

TESS. Nothing it's just – someone asked me when I first learned that sexuality could be used as a tool and that's. Probably it

LOUIS. What do you mean "someone"? You mean the client questionnaire?

TESS. Oh. Well yeah

LOUIS. Have you Taken the client questionnaire? Maybe that's why you're such a star employee

TESS. Hardly

LOUIS. I'm serious. I did data entry for a bunch of your clients this morning. You're crushing it

TESS. What, are they getting "fast-tracked"?

LOUIS. Some of them, yeah. Or else scoring higher than they ever have

TESS. *(Unenthused.)* Cool.

LOUIS. "Cool"?

TESS. It's not a big deal

LOUIS. Yes it is

TESS. It's really not

LOUIS. Come on. Own it

TESS. Whatever

LOUIS. *(Psh.)* What's up with you? You're making moves newbie

>*(They "cheers" with their punch cups. Short beat and then:)*

Truth or dare

TESS. Whaaaat

LOUIS. Your story brought me back

TESS. What are we twelve?

LOUIS. Come on, truth or dare

TESS. …

Truth

LOUIS. Okay ummm. Fuck marry kill: the three founders

TESS. Wow all right

>*(Considers.)*

Fuck…Dr. Quill. She's got that mysterious vibe

LOUIS. You mean that she's always MIA

TESS. Also that. So if it went terribly we'd barely have to see each other again

LOUIS. Smart

TESS. Marry…Dr. Foggstein, aka Mandy. Feel like my life would be really organized. So I guess that leaves /

LOUIS. *(!)* Kill Natalia? Cold

TESS. Hey it's the game. Truth or dare

LOUIS. Truth

(**TESS** *considers. For a moment.*)

TESS. What do you hate most about this job?

LOUIS. Ummmm

(*Considers.*)

Data entry? Or doubles. Yeah. Data entry or doubles. It's a tie

TESS. (*Disappointed...*) That's it?

LOUIS. What do you mean? It's a cushy gig, as you know

TESS. I kind of feel like I keep waiting for it to get better

LOUIS. (*...?*) You're kicking ass

TESS. But what does that mean exactly

LOUIS. That you'll probably be eligible for a raise soon

TESS. In terms of clients

LOUIS. I think you know what it means in terms of clients

TESS. Okay yes, they're getting vulnerable, they're apologizing

LOUIS. Exactly

TESS. They're doing some soul-searching, their eyes are opening. But

LOUIS. ...But

TESS. I don't know. I figured it would feel like, a balm

LOUIS. A bomb?

TESS. A balm

LOUIS. Like (*Makes an explosion noise.*)?

TESS. No a *balm*. Like, lotion

LOUIS. (*...*) You expected it to feel like lotion

TESS. I expected to feel something, seismic?

LOUIS. Woah

TESS. Or something, I don't know, freeing? I expected to feel

Something

LOUIS. Like success

TESS. Like vindication

LOUIS. You don't feel vindicated?

TESS. For a millisecond. And then – [ ]

LOUIS. And then... You remember you have health insurance? And benefits? And free CrossFit classes? And free acai bowls? And a hefty paycheck? And a 401k? And the ability to actually build a life for yourself in this capitalist hellhole of a city?

TESS. I mean. Yes. All true Yes /

LOUIS. This is the best job I've ever had

Truth or Dare

TESS. ...Dare

LOUIS. I dare you to yell something at the top of your lungs

TESS. What

LOUIS. In five, / four

TESS. Ahh wait!

LOUIS. Three, two, one!

> (**TESS** *yells something at the top of her lungs.*)
>
> (*They laugh.*)

TESS. Truth or dare

LOUIS. Dare

TESS. I dare you to stand on that table

LOUIS. That table?

TESS. That table

>   (**LOUIS** *looks at the table.*)

>   (*Then, he stands on top of it. Dances a little.*)

>   (*Until:*)

NATALIA. *(Offstage.)* Louis what are you doing / [?]

>   (**LOUIS** *hops off.*)

>   (**TESS** *and* **LOUIS** *crack up.*)

LOUIS. Truth or dare

TESS. Dare

LOUIS. I dare you to /

>   (**TESS** *kisses* **LOUIS.**)

>   (*But* **LOUIS** *backs away.*)

Um

TESS. Oh

Oh god

LOUIS. Sorry /

TESS. No I'm, *I'm* sorry

LOUIS. ...We're co-workers

TESS. Right yes

LOUIS. So this would be Really / unprofessional

TESS. Unprofessional, of course. *(Actually sobering up.)* I'm super drunk right now I'm sorry

LOUIS. It's okay it's just, I'm kind of seeing someone

TESS. Oh oh my god Yeah that's, Great. Yeah

LOUIS. If I gave you the impression that / I

TESS. No no it's fine

LOUIS. It's kind of my / personality to

TESS. Totally fine.

LOUIS. But I always draw a line, that's something I always do: draw a line

TESS. Right

> *(Awkward beat.)*

You're one of the few people who makes this place bearable. I just figured maybe you'd make me

feel

[bearable]

> *(Another awkward beat.)*

LOUIS. I don't mean any offense or anything but, a person can't be your

balm. You know that right?

TESS. What

LOUIS. I can't be your

balm

> *(Lights.)*

> *(**TESS** alone, on the phone.)*

TESS. Hi... Oh no I'm fine I'm fine! Sorry to freak you out. I just wanted to hear your – ...Well we never said Zero Contact that's... But you picked up... I'm just saying, you didn't have to pick up but you did, right? So... Work is good. It's. Really Good. Everyone's a genius here... Uh-huh, so many brilliant thinkers and scientists and... It's beautiful... My apartment's on a street lined with palm trees... No I didn't just call you to – How are You? ...That's great... No I mean it, that's great. You seem Great... I'm still at work. We had this, Halloween party here tonight so... Exactly, it's really social which is... Yeah... No no I'm about to leave I just needed a minute to

...

It's hard. It's actually really – ...Here. At this... It's hard to be steeped in all these – Like I have to relive all these – All these moments I didn't fully grasp at the time? Like I didn't have the language, or the awareness to grasp them? I just knew I felt a certain way and I figured that was the way I was meant to feel and now I'm back Inside the moments and I'm thinking, *god* I didn't actually have to... Oh no I understand... Yeah I know it's late there... Sure sure I'm sorry to – ...You too. Have a good /

7.

(Lights.)

(An examination room.)

*(**TESS** and **JACKSON**.)*

JACKSON. So. This is it. The home stretch

TESS. Yep

JACKSON. Bottom of the ninth. Bases loaded

TESS. Sure

JACKSON. Not big on sports metaphors?

TESS. I was never much of an athlete

JACKSON. You know the best part of Varsity soccer was when they gave out awards, at the end

TESS. *(Unenthused.)* Sounds

nice

JACKSON. So do we get any?

TESS. Excuse me?

JACKSON. I finished my "season" at The Gradient, right? So do I get an award? It's okay if you don't have a plaque or anything

TESS. *(Barely playing along.)* Yeah, there was a mix-up with the plaque deliveries. We'll mail it to you

JACKSON. I'll keep an eye out for it. What is it though? The award

TESS. ...Team Spirit

JACKSON. Ooh that was always a bad one. That was always code for like, you cheer loudly from the bench

TESS. Well maybe you can try again next season

JACKSON. True. Wait, next season?

TESS. I just mean there's always a chance that clients return

JACKSON. *(Aww.)* Are you banking on me coming back? Are you hoping that we cross paths again?

TESS. I'm trying to help you be realistic about your future

JACKSON. All right, Miss Practical

(*Catching self.) Ms.* Ms. Practical

TESS. *(Let's get this show on the road.)* I'm going to ask you a series of closing questions. Okay, 5247?

JACKSON. Hang on, how do I make sure I'm assigned to you if I do come back?

TESS. That's, not something we can control

JACKSON. Even when we're a team?

TESS. ...We're not a team

JACKSON. Of course we're a team. Dynamic duo over here. You're my secret weapon. They're gonna make little action figures out of us. Kids will be lining up in toy stores

TESS. Yeah, I'm trying to picture this and it's just not, it's not there

JACKSON. No but seriously, we did this together. You Fast Tracked me

TESS. That wasn't me, that was the algorithm

JACKSON. I mean, it wasn't Not you

TESS. *(Rattled.)* It wasn't me.

(*Back to business.)* I'm going to ask you a series of closing questions, okay Jackson?

JACKSON. *(Realizing.)* Did you just use my name?

TESS. ...No

JACKSON. Yeah you did, you just used my name. Instead of my I.D. number

TESS. *(Back to business.)* #5247, How would you describe how you're feeling right now?

JACKSON. I'm feeling... I'm feeling relaxed

TESS. Okay

JACKSON. And – at ease. Yeah, at ease.

TESS. Relaxed and at ease. Okay

> *(She marks this down.)*

Anything else to add?

JACKSON. No I think that sums it up.

TESS. Can you please walk me through some of the tangible skills that you feel you've gained during your time here?

JACKSON. Uhhh. I've learned about active listening. And about not taking up too much space. Or too much air. Ummm. I've learned what makes a good apology, and what makes a shitty one. I've learned how to be less calculating, and more empathic. I've learned how to lead with respect instead of with flirtation. Do you want me to say / [more?]

TESS. No this should work fine. Thank you

> *(**TESS** marks some things down.)*

JACKSON. How am I doing so far?

TESS. How are you doing?

JACKSON. Yeah, how's this going? Going okay?

TESS. Your data isn't even being aggregated. This is basically a formality

JACKSON. *("That's my girl.")* Tess, always keeping me in the loop

TESS. It's not like it's a secret

JACKSON. So this is just, for us?

TESS. *(?)* For / [us]

JACKSON. Giving us the space to say our goodbyes? That's nice. I'm glad they carve out the time

TESS. We also have the right to quote some of your responses and use them for marketing purposes

JACKSON. *(Some kind of joke...??)* Aren't you supposed to get my Consent. For that type of thing

TESS. We already got your consent, when you arrived. I put it in your packet of welcome documents on the first day

JACKSON. Ohhh right

Well I was a little distracted

TESS. *(?)* By

JACKSON. You.

TESS. ...

JACKSON. Come on, you know that you're distracting. That pretty smile? Distracting

TESS. *(Uncomfortable.)* Okay, why don't / we

JACKSON. Don't tell me that's off limits. Commenting on an objective fact? That can't be off limits

TESS. I wouldn't call that an ob/jective fact

JACKSON. You're obviously Aware that you have a gorgeous / smile

TESS. Yeah, okay / let's

JACKSON. What am I making you uncomfortable?

TESS. *(Yes.)* No, I'm just /

JACKSON. It's an observation, that's all

TESS. Okay we don't need to dwell / on

JACKSON. In my humble opinion / you have an

TESS. Yeah we don't / need to

JACKSON. Amazing smile

TESS. *(Not enjoying this.)* Thank you. Thank. You. *(Back to business.)* Can you please describe one memorable moment during your time here?

JACKSON. Any moment at all?

TESS. Any moment that sticks out to you

> *(**JACKSON** looks at **TESS**.)*
>
> *(**TESS** looks back.)*
>
> *(And then:)*

JACKSON. That first night, in my pod, was pretty bleak. Those pods are – They're depressing as hell. One window. One droopy cot. Some generic, like, stupid-fucking photograph on the wall. One of those photographs that comes with the picture frame when you buy it – I think it was a sailboat. It was bleak.

> *(**TESS** records his response.)*
>
> *(He considers her.)*
>
> *(For a moment.)*

(Considering her.) Something's wrong

TESS. With / [?]

JACKSON. The way you just recorded that response – you didn't like it. Something's wrong

TESS. *(?)* Nothing's wrong

JACKSON. *(He's got it.)* Wait a second, wait a second. You thought I was going to describe a moment that involved *you*!

TESS. That's insane

JACKSON. No no no your whole self-deprecating, whatever. I'm making it worse

TESS. *(?)* What are you even – I don't care / what you

JACKSON. But you do care. Of course you care. I make a comment about your smile and your whole day turns around. It's slight but I still see it.

(**TESS** *makes a decision.*)

TESS. There has been a mistake in the algorithm's calculations

JACKSON. *(Amused.)* Oh yeah?

TESS. This is not your exit interview. That was reported in error. This is routine processing

JACKSON. Really pulling out all the stops aren't you

TESS. It has become increasingly apparent that you have learned nothing during your time here

JACKSON. That's a little harsh

TESS. That you have demonstrated zero development or growth

JACKSON. Now that's just an exaggeration

TESS. And that you are unfit for re-entry

JACKSON. And what are you going to do about that?

TESS. I'm going to report you. You talked about reporting me, I can report you too

JACKSON. And then what

TESS. And then you stay here. Indefinitely

JACKSON. Indefinitely?

TESS. Yes. Indefinitely.

JACKSON. See, this is what you all don't seem to get: That people like Me determine the value of So much in this world – and that includes you. You Need me to tell you who you are and what you're worth. People like me will you into existence. And you pretend to hate that, but you've structured your whole being around my approval. You're constantly craving it. So all this? This is just, dressing. Decoration. Because you, and the entire world, are never going to change. Do you understand?

> (**JACKSON** *touches* **TESS**.)
>
> (*As if to comfort her.*)
>
> (*Or will her into existence.*)
>
> (*She recoils.*)

Tess…?

TESS. …

I know so many Jacksons.

JACKSON. Yeah…it's kind of a popular name

TESS. I've met you one thousand times. You think you Know me? You think you See me? You think I Care about you? You think I Want you to care about Me? Do you know what I want? Do you know what I actually want, when I look at you? I want to reach inside your throat and claw your esophagus. I want to crush your liver into a very very fine paste. I want to cut your spleen into six different pieces and then shove them up your colon. I want to deflate your fucking lungs, I want to pulverize your fucking penis, I want to sever your spinal cord and I want to shatter every single one of your bones and I can. I can do that. With my bare hands, I can do that

People don't expect that of me But I am REALLY CAPABLE OKAY? I am capable OF A LOT I am capable of MULTITUDES and I'm not gonna SETTLE FOR THIS SHIT You think you KNOW me? You don't even have the LANGUAGE for all that I am! I am more powerful than you can even UNDERSTAND Your brain CAN'T EVEN COMPUTE MY POWER! Because I have more drive and more dignity and more wit and more grace and more sex appeal and more charisma and more imagination and more intelligence than you can COMPREHEND! You should be QUOTING ME you should be

STUDYING ME IN LECTURE HALLS you should be BOWING DOWN TO ME you should BE SO LUCKY TO BE NEAR ME BECAUSE I AM A RADIANT VISIONARY GENIUS AND YOU CAN'T TOUCH ME YOU CAN'T AFFECT ME I'M IMPENETRABLE AND YOU ARE NOTHING

(A moment.)

(And then...)

A VERY SOOTHING VOICE.   Hello there. Pardon the interruption. We just wanted to remind everyone that The Gradient does not endorse violence, or aggression, or rage in any shape or form. Because here at The Gradient, we believe it's important to maintain perspective. And composure. And generally to: Calm Down.

So, Tess? Hello there? Tess? Please gather your belongings and report to security. *(Gruff.)* Immediately. *(Suddenly cheery yoga teacher.)* Thank you. And Namaste.

   (Darkness.)

   (And then...)

8.

(The Gradient offices.)

(Tess is nowhere to be found. There isn't a trace of her.)

(It's just NATALIA and LOUIS.)

(They sip coffee.)

(A regular day.)

(Slow.)

NATALIA. I can't believe the machine in the lobby's broken.

> *(Sip.)*

I feel like I'm drinking lighter fluid.

> *(Sip.)*

LOUIS. I can't really taste the difference

NATALIA. Seriously?

LOUIS. Caffeine is caffeine is caffeine.

> *(Biiiig sip.)*

NATALIA. Woah, easy

LOUIS. I'm in the middle of a double

NATALIA. Oh. Godspeed.

> *(Sip sip.)*

You should eat something.

LOUIS. I stole some tuna steak from the Silicon Valley bros.

NATALIA. They're so bougie.

> *(They laugh.)*

(Sip.)

(Sip.)

NATALIA. Can't wait 'til Sunday.

LOUIS. Me too.

NATALIA. Cannot Wait.

LOUIS. What're you gonna do

NATALIA. Work on my pottery

LOUIS. You still do that?

NATALIA. What do you mean do I Still Do That? It's my passion

LOUIS. Sorry, sorry. Shitty memory

NATALIA. Yeah whatever.

(Sip.)

(Sip.)

(Sip.)

I made a coil pot, last weekend.

LOUIS. Oh yeah?

NATALIA. Yeah

LOUIS. What's that again

NATALIA. It's the one where you take your slab roller, and you roll out the clay, and then you cut it into long strips, and then you knead the strips into coils. And then you pinch them together and stack them on top of each other. And you just keep stacking.

LOUIS. Ah. How big was your pot

NATALIA. Almost four feet

LOUIS. Woah what?

NATALIA. I just kept stacking the coils. Stacking and stacking. And the sun was coming through the window. And no one was telling me to stop.

It collapsed – the pot collapsed. Wouldn't have fit in my kiln anyway, but.

(Sip.)

(Sip.)

God I live for Sundays.

When I retire, I think I'm just going to make coil pots, all day long

And eat like, really beautiful salads.

I don't know. Something, simple. That I can control.

Something

Safe.

(Blackout.)

End of Play

www.ingramcontent.com/pod-product-compliance
Lightning Source LLC
Chambersburg PA
CBHW070343120726
47909CB00008B/2730